With special thanks to the original
surfing fairy Johnny Davies

Emma Thomson's
*felicity Wishes*®

FELICITY WISHES: MAKE-UP MAGIC
by Emma Thomson

British Library Cataloguing in Publication Data
A catalogue record of this book is available from the British Library.
ISBN 0-340-88185-2
Felicity Wishes © 2000 Emma Thomson.
Licensed by White Lion Publishing.
Felicity Wishes: Make-up Magic © 2004 Emma Thomson.

First HB edition published 2004
10 9 8 7 6 5 4 3 2 1

Published by Hodder Children's Books, a division of Hodder Headline Limited,
338 Euston Road, London, NW1 3BH

Printed in China

# Emma Thomson's felicity Wishes®

# Make-up Magic

Hodder Children's Books

A division of Hodder Headline Limited

Felicity Wishes and her fairy friends, Holly and Polly, were sitting in the warm summer sun when Daisy appeared waving an envelope in her hand.

"I've won!" she called excitedly.

"Won what?" asked Felicity, squinting at Daisy over the top of her sunglasses.

"I entered a competition in 'Fairy Girl' magazine and I've won a free photo-shoot," said Daisy. "And the best part of it is that you can all come too!"

Suddenly, the quiet park erupted with fairy giggles and excited squeals.

"We'll have to look our best," said Holly. "And how better to do it than with a magic touch of fairy make-up."

Within minutes, Felicity and her friends were shopping in Fairy Glamour, the make-up shop on the High Street.

"I never know which make-up to choose," said Felicity looking puzzled.

"I always want it all!" said Polly picking up various types of lipgloss.

"And I always buy the same make-up because I know it suits me," said Daisy joining in.

"Don't worry, I know everything there is to know about make-up," said Holly as she started to fill her basket with lots of glittery bottles and twinkly jars.

## HOLLY'S TOP TIPS

♥ If you want some advice about choosing the right type of make-up ask an assistant.

♥ Spend time looking for the right make-up.

♥ Get together with a friend and try out different colours on each other.

♥ When testing colours in a shop, use your face instead of your hand.

When the fairies reached Fairy Photos,
Holly's wings were feeling the strain of
all the make-up she had bought.

The receptionist led them into the pinkest,
plushest dressing room they had ever seen. "Feel free
to borrow our 'Fairy Make-up Manual'," she said.

"Some of us don't need it," said Holly as she
closed the curtains of the private dressing room with
a dramatic swish.

Felicity, Polly and Daisy sat in front of the
main dressing table and turned the first page of
the manual.

"Oooh! Twinkly
blusher secrets,"
squealed Daisy.

# Blusher Secrets

Blusher is available in powder or cream.

When applying blusher, brush up and out from the centre of your cheek with light strokes.

Blend the colour well towards the hairline so you avoid harsh edges.

## TIPS FOR YOU

♥ Use a large brush for a soft look.

♥ Don't put too much blusher on your cheeks. Remember less is definitely more.

♥ If you have no blusher, dot a touch of pink lipstick on your cheeks and blend it in well.

♥ Use soft colours in pink or peach.

# Eyeshadow Hints

If you have blue or grey eyes, yellow or orange eyeshadow will work well.

If you have green eyes, plum coloured eyeshadow will make your eyes stand out.

To emphasise brown eyes, use pink eyeshadow.

Felicity, Polly and Daisy put the finishing touches to their blusher and eagerly turned the next page of the manual.

"Glittery eye make-up!" said Polly clapping her hands excitedly.

"Look at the wonderful effects you can get with just the tiniest touch of eyeshadow," said Daisy.

"I never knew fairy eyes could look so beautiful," said Felicity. "We must show Holly or she'll miss out," she said walking towards the private room.

"Not yet!" Holly sang. "I don't want to spoil the surprise!"

There was only one thing left for the fairies to do before they were ready for their photo-shoot.

"Shimmery lips!" said Felicity, tipping the contents of her fairy glamour bag onto the table.

There were so many lipglosses to choose from. "Let's try them all!" said Polly excitedly.

"Not at the same time!" giggled Felicity.

"Hmmm," agreed Daisy. "It says in the manual that 'less is more' and that it is the little glittery touches that make you a beautiful fairy."

# How to have
# Lovely Lips

### ♥ NATURAL
The easiest way to make your lips look natural is to choose a shade of pink and cover with lipgloss.

### ♥ PARTY LOOK
If you really want to shine, add glitter gloss over the top of your favourite lipstick!

### ♥ STAY PUT
Press your lips together on a tissue after you have applied lipstick, then add another coat. It will last longer.

### ♥ OWN STYLE
Mix and match lipsticks to create your own colour.

Cream

Admiring their new look, the three fairies swivelled in their chairs with excitement.

"We're ready when you are," they called to Holly.

"Nearly there," cried Holly in a flustered voice. "I just can't decide between orange and green eyeshadow or pink and yellow!" she said pulling back the curtain.

Daisy and Polly held back their giggles.

"Perhaps," offered Felicity, trying not to hurt Holly's feelings, "we could try the page in the manual on make-up removal?"

## MAKE-UP REMOVAL TIPS

♥ Removing make-up before you go to bed will leave your skin clean and soft.

♥ Use a gentle cleanser to get rid of every bit of make-up.

♥ Use a cotton bud soaked in cleanser to remove make-up under your eyelashes.

spray away

Wish Wash Wipe

Cream

After persuading Holly that a natural look was far from boring, the fairies set to work on her new make-up.

When the fairies made their grand entrance into the studio, the photographer beamed. "You all look wonderful! But you've forgotten one thing."

The fairies looked at each other blankly.

"Star dust, of course," said the photographer as she sprinkled each of the fairies in a shower of twinkly glitter.

"Smile," she said as she snapped the camera. But Felicity and her friends were already smiling.

Strike a pose!

Love the camera!

Smile!

A few weeks later, Felicity, Holly and Polly were having hot chocolate in Sparkles cafe when Daisy burst through the door in excitement.

"Look!" she said opening her bag and taking out a large package. "Our photos have arrived and, even more exciting, they've updated the 'Fairy Make-up Manual' with our photos!"

The fairies couldn't believe their eyes.

"Wow!" said Felicity with a smile. "It's amazing what magic just a little make-up can do!"

# FAIRY MAKE-UP MANUAL

## MAGIC MAKE-UP TIPS

When first using make-up, look in a mirror and identify different parts of your face.

Make sure your face is freshly washed before you apply make-up.

You don't need to wear a lot of make-up to dazzle, but you do need a smile!

Remember if you over paint your face, you could end up looking more like a clown than a fairy!

Apply make-up under a good light.

Less is more!

With this make-up
book comes an extra sparkly
Felicity wish:

Open this book with your eyes closed
and let it fall open on any page.
Think of a wish you always dreamed
would come true and whisper it into
the page three times.

Keep this book in a safe place and,
maybe, one day, your wish
might just come true.

Love *felicity*
x